Stella's Christmas Family Tree

M.B. O'Reilly

ISBN 978-1-7392134-1-1

For Conor, without whose support, moral, and most definitely technical, this would still be a plain old Word document.

As Stella sat and read beside the sparkling Christmas tree,

She heard a knock, the doorbell rang – ding, dong! – who could it be?

She scrambled to her feet and quickly slid across the floor,

And faster than old Santa's sleigh she flew towards the door.

She turned the key and pulled the heavy bolt back with a clank

And there she saw – a snowman? – Oh no, wait - it's Uncle Frank!

"Come in! Come in!" she called and Uncle Frank stamped on the mat.

He shook and brushed the snow from off his jacket, gloves and hat.

He shook and brushed the snow from off his trousers, shoes and socks,

And just then Stella noticed that her uncle had a box.

A curious box, more like a case, long and black and thin.

"This is for you!" beamed Uncle Frank and gave a hearty grin.

Stella's eyes surveyed the box from narrow end to wide

And couldn't quite imagine what she'd hope to find inside.

"Thank you, Uncle Frank!" she said "But really, don't you know

That usually the gifts you bring are wrapped up with a bow?"

"Aha!" laughed Uncle Frank and then he sat her on his knee.

"There isn't any wrapping but there is a bow, just see!"

With twinkling eyes he smiled at Stella, filled with Christmas joy.

He tapped the box and said, "This gift is better than a toy."

And just like a magician, he put his hand within

And pulled out – not a rabbit – but a shiny violin.

"Wow!" gasped Stella, gazing at the dark and glossy wood.

She asked if she could hold it and her uncle said she could.

"But," said her uncle, "Listen! There is something you should know.

There's something quite unique about this violin and bow.

Then Uncle Frank said:

"It's older than you; it's older than me.
It's made from the wood of our family tree.

It plays songs of our family, songs of our clan,
Our stories and songs since our family began."

So Stella, very carefully, picked up the violin
And tucked it closely in between her shoulder and her chin.
She pulled the bow across the strings and as she played the note
She felt her fingers tingle and her feet began to float.
Then she, along with Uncle Frank, was lifted up and swirled
And set back down again into a rather different world.

The lights were low and noisy children chattered with delight,
A little tree with cones and berries glowed in candle light.
The children's clothes looked very odd, like costumes in a play:
Not at all the sort of clothes that people wear today.
A mother sitting writing and an old man in a chair,
A plate of sliced-up fruit cake for the family to share.
Stella looked but couldn't see a phone or a TV –
The children so delighted just to watch the Christmas tree.
Then Stella said, "The tree's so very tiny and what's more,
They're acting like they've never seen a Christmas tree before."

She couldn't understand and Uncle Frank replied with glee,
"Well, it IS the first time ever that they've seen a Christmas tree.
The year is 1860 and in those olden days
They celebrated Christmas in rather different ways.
No one thought to decorate a tree with bells and lights
Or gather round its glowing warmth on cold December nights,
Until Prince Albert, Queen Victoria's husband, had the plan
To do just that and that's how the tradition first began.

Stella gazed in wonder and surveyed this special place,
The scent of roasting chestnuts and the joy on every face.
The smells, the sights, then all at once, from over in the chair,
Her ears were filled with music that was wafting through the air.

The strings of violin were playing music so entrancing
That everyone was moved and started singing, hugging, dancing.
And Stella too was tapping 'til she looked down at her hand –
Her violin had disappeared – she didn't understand.
"Uncle, where's my violin? I had it only now.
It vanished in an instant and I really don't know how.

And Uncle Frank, gently swaying like the Christmas tree,

Said, "Stella, that old violin is part of you and me.

But it started long before us. You see, look over there!

It's playing in the hands of that old fellow in the chair.

He's your great, great grandfather, with lots of 'greats' on top.

He played **their** "Merry Christmas" and still it doesn't stop.

And as he plays his melody and everybody sings,

Every note he played is still remembered in the strings.

Remember, Stella, that violin

Is older than you; it's older than me.

It's made from the wood of our family tree.

It plays songs of our family, songs of our clan,

Our stories and songs since our family began."

The music now grows quieter; the haunting tune still lingers,
When Stella was aware of something pressing at her fingers.
The violin back in her hand, a sudden whirlwind swirled
And lifted them above that unfamiliar Christmas world.
It carried them a little way; it didn't take them far;
And set them down into a scene which also seemed bizarre.
A little girl, curled in a chair, gave her doll a hug,
While two more older children played at marbles on the rug.

Beyond them, in the kitchen, their mum prepared to fry
The onions she had sliced and which she said had made her cry.
The parsnips and potatoes, which were scarce, were chopped and peeled,
While cooking in the oven was a rabbit from the field.
The sugar, which was gold-dust, and the butter had been laid
On the table in the kitchen for the pudding to be made.

The radio was humming and Stella heard it say
"Best wishes to our listeners! A Merry Christmas Day!"
Stella frowned. "But, Uncle Frank, there's holly on the wall
But apart from that you wouldn't think it's Christmas Day at all."
"This family will feast, remembering what this day is for,
But the year is 1914 and the country is at war.
Their father's in the army – he's miles and miles away.
He won't be home to feast and celebrate with them today.
Even Christmas dinner will be simpler than it should
Because of all the rationing and shortages of food.

But they're keeping spirits up and dispelling all the gloom,"
And at that moment music rose within that quiet room.
Stella saw the violin, the movement of the bow,
The harmony produced as it was guided to and fro.
The eldest girl was playing it, her pigtails brushed aside,
The younger children sang along and mum looked on with pride.
"That's your auntie (great, great, great), the tune she plays is splendid.
The violin remembers even when her tune has ended.
They sing of fields and shepherds watching sheep by starry light,
While loved-ones off in fields in France were singing 'Silent Night'.

Yes, that violin

Is older than you; it's older than me.
It's made from the wood of our family tree.

It plays songs of our family, songs of our clan,
Our stories and songs since our family began."

The music now grows soft again and Stella is aware
That the gently-swaying melody is hanging in the air.
Violin in hand again, the visitors are lifted
By breezes swirling round and once again their world is shifted.

It swirls them and it twirls them and before their very eyes
They're in a place that Uncle Frank and Stella recognise.
A silent place, no cars at all, and all along the street
The silence only broken by a chatty robin's tweet.

"I know this place!" cried Stella, "It's your street and there's your door
With the funny lion knocker which I've knocked upon before.
The rainbow in the window and the little face-masked gnome.
Is our adventure finished now? Are we going home?"

"We're very close to home, " he said. "It's not too far away.

Now the music's brought us to a recent Christmas Day.

A Christmas not so long ago when all across the nation

Christmas celebrations were disturbed by isolation.

People couldn't travel far and people couldn't mingle
And jingle bells and Christmas tills all found it hard to jingle."
Just then a strange thing happened, like magic had been done –
Another Uncle Frank appeared – two instead of one!
An Uncle Frank beside her and another over there,
Identical (except his clothes and slightly longer hair).
The violin was in **his** hand; the winter chill grew colder;
He lifted it and delicately placed it on his shoulder.
And in that bleak midwinter, he played a rousing song,
And merrily on high the Christmas bells rang out – ding, dong!
The music swept along and entered every neighbour's ear
And one-by-one, those unknown neighbours started to appear.
Doors unlocked and opened up and every person gave
A friendly smile, a cheery nod, a 'Merry Christmas' wave.
And for a moment, time stood still, frozen like the weather
And everyone rejoiced and from a distance came together.

Stella too was humming as that Uncle Frank was playing.
The Uncle Frank beside her turned and smiled and started saying,

"That violin

Is older than you; it's older than me.
It's made from the wood of our family tree.

It plays songs of our family, songs of our clan,
Our stories and songs since our family began."

Then all at once, the breezes blew, the Christmas snowflakes swirled
And Stella and her uncle were transported from that world.

In just an eye-blink they were home, and with a happy grin,

Stella saw there, in her hand, the family violin.

"It's just the best gift ever; I'll never let it go.

Thank you, thank you, thank you for this violin and bow."

"Well," said Uncle Frank, "You have seen its curious mystery.

Now you can play and play your part in adding to its history.

It plays and it remembers, in each and every string,

The magic of our music and the story that we bring."

About the Author

M.B. O'Reilly studied Classics at the University of Glasgow and went on to complete a PhD there on Ovid's Metamorphoses. After a brief foray into public sector accounting, she decided to undertake the PGCE teacher training course where her interest in creative writing, particularly story-telling through rhyme, was sparked. She taught Latin for several years before stepping back to be at home with her boys. During that time, she published Tales from Olympus, a collection of stories from Greek and Roman myth. She is currently teaching Latin again, still writing (and illustrating!) and working on various projects to widen access to Classical subjects in secondary schools.
She lives in Glasgow with her husband and three cheeky (and permanently hungry) boys.

www.mboreilly.com
@MB_OReilly

Images by:

M.B.O'Reilly
brgfx/ Freepik
fanjianhua/Freepik
Freepik
Ikaika/Freepik
katemangostar/Freepik
macrovector/Freepik
pchvector/Freepik
pikisuperstar/Freepik
rawpixel.com/Freepik
upklyak/Freepik

Printed in Great Britain
by Amazon